MELVILLE MANIFESTOS

A MODEST PROPOSAL

MELVILLE HOUSE PUBLISHING
HOBOKEN, NEW JERSEY

RÉGIS DEBRAY

A MODEST PROPOSAL

A PLAN FOR THE GOLDEN YEARS

TRANSLATED BY JEFFREY MEHLMAN

BOOK DESIGN: DAVID KONOPKA

MELVILLE HOUSE PUBLISHING
300 OBSERVER HIGHWAY
THIRD FLOOR
HOBOKEN, NJ 07030

FIRST MELVILLE HOUSE PRINTING · MAY 2006
ISBN 10: 1-933633-03-4
ISBN 13: 978-1-933633-03-9

PRINTED IN CANADA

A CATALOG RECORD FOR THIS BOOK IS
AVAILABLE FROM THE LIBRARY OF CONGRESS.

CONTENTS

A MODEST PROPOSAL

FOREWORD

Old age is a new idea in Europe, and the waning of a sense of the future is a matter of some concern in our various nations. When the long term atrophies under pressure of urgency, the civic sense ends up knowing a comparable fate under the sickly sweet despotism of edifying sentiments.

It is for that reason, Mr. President, that you have entrusted to me, in agreement with the Economic and Social Council, the imposing task of breaking free of the emotions of the day in order to reflect on measures intended to avert the assorted shipwrecks that await us. It occurs to me that you did so neither with an eye to the year of my birth alone nor in response to a certain penchant for defending lost causes—the only ones worthy of a gentleman—but because a philosopher by training is better equipped than others, say, sociologists or historians, to adopt the perspective of the whole in relation to the part, and that of the future in relation to the present. You have proposed that I do my duty in strictest conformity with reason alone, based on available statistics and the current state of the data, without yielding to that vain wish to *please*, whose bitter sequels are all too familiar to us. I hope not to disappoint your expectations concerning this last point, aware as I am that one must on occasion, in the short term, dishearten both the wealthy suburbanites of Neuilly and the workers of Billancourt if one is to clear the way for the sustained growth that will be of benefit to them both.

Yours is the exalted mission of enlightening the initiatives of a government tending too often to be short-sighted and accommodating, inhibited as it is by routine, initial impulse, and the defense of privilege. My task is assuredly easier: to sketch the rather steep path (without condemning *a priori* more apparently gentle slopes) toward the society of free choice which all of us wholeheartedly desire, and in which every individual will be able to live, work, and die as he wants, but to which no approach, let it be acknowledged, will be painless. What measure of sacrifice will we accept? It will fall to our European leaders, in the social policy regarding old age that I am calling to your attention, to draw the line between what is desirable and what is possible.

It is a commonplace that a good visionary does not make for a good administrator, and vice versa. Being neither one nor the other, I will not expose myself to that classic incongruity. For the happiness of a citizen among others it suffices that he contribute his brick to the collective construction of the future, whatever the damage to the prejudices, interests, and accommodations which any insight in advance of its time can not fail to unsettle.

I.

THE PROBLEMS

Eighty-two years for women, seventy-four for men. Just how far will our society extend its lack of medical awareness, its economic irresponsibility? Our government will have no end of its rush over the cliff of onerous taxation without *first of all* finding a remedy for the accelerated aging of the population, whose intolerable preponderance eliminates all possibility of return to greater stability as to a lost social dynamic. How indeed are we to "force a retreat from poverty and mistreatment" if at the same time death continues to outpace us, if the growth rate of the inactive, aged segment of the population persists in being double that of the active sector, if the tens of centenarians whom the France of 1950 sheltered turn into hundreds of thousands in 2050? We are confronting the sieve-like cask of the mythological daughters of Danaus.

The reform of health insurance, the re-examination of reimbursements, the swelling of retirement funds, the extension of the period of premium payments, the computerization of individual medical records: the pettiness of all such tinkering only masks the real challenge, which is to absorb an imminent demographic shock. Ever-expanding life spans augment deficits and impinge negatively on every prospect of budgetary remedy. The key to recovery is also the bolt that keeps it locked out of reach because it involves a taboo. Were it not that universal suffrage constrains the political class to resort to a puerile combination of good will and bad faith, our fellow citizens would long since have realized that we have already reached flood level.

A few statistics: life expectancy at birth grows by a year every five years. From sixteen years for sixty-year old men and twenty-one years for women, in 1970, it is expected to climb, in 2020, to twenty-three and twenty-eight years respectively. Currently capped at age 106, the age limit of mortality charts for life insurance could reach 130 or 150 in a few decades. Statisticians estimate that in France, in 2020, individuals over 60 will outnumber those under 20. In Europe, the continent counting the largest proportion of aged individuals, old age is synonymous with retirement. Whereas one old duffer out of ten, in the France of 1900, if he had the good fortune to be a railway employee, teacher, or postman, received a pension in 1900—the remainder having to either squirrel away savings in anticipation, in the case of the industrious, or throw themselves on the mercy of public charity, in that of the tattered and indigent—there are no longer any wage-earners today without claims to a pension, even as the length of retirements has doubled over the last fifty years. It is common knowledge, moreover, that health-related expenses increase with age. One third of all prescriptions are issued to the oldest 10 percent of the population, a category that takes, on the average, eight medications daily. Plans for universal health coverage attribute an extraordinary spirit of sacrifice to future tax-payers, so great is the gap, in this case more than in others, between consumption and available income. The state can not do everything, which is even less the case with an annual increase of 1.5 percent in the gross domestic product, and the capacities of our hospitals have their limits.

With the new prestige of "solidarity-oriented socializing," moreover, the retirement years go together, in most cases, with a renewal of activities that are not only sporting in nature (fishing, golf, walking, canoeing, etc.), but benevolent and even humanitarian. Far from withdrawing to the shadows, new retirees are on the lookout for every fissure in the commercial sector (emeritus status, honorific appointments in various associations, foundations, NGOs, etc.) allowing them to make their way back, without the slightest embarrassment and occasionally incognito into active life—a sympathetic form of cheating (jobs for the old!), but concerning which newcomers to the job market may have every reason to complain.

To the very extent that the aged, in periods of sustained growth, present the attraction of their potential as consumers, thanks in particular to the established system of assistance and protection, when the growth rate fails to exceed a paltry 2 percent, they mean delayed recovery, aggravated public debt (already approaching a billion euros), loss of control over expenditures, a damper on technological development and innovation, and finally a decline in the standard of living. The upkeep of dependents has come perilously close to costing each and every citizen the equivalent of one day off annually. Agreeing to an ever-increasing financial outlay for a portion of the population whose social usefulness diminishes by the day cannot be taken for granted. Neither a procreator nor a creator of wealth, the less the aged subject proves useful to society, the more he costs it. To be sure he is adept at saving his money: those older than fifty possess 60 percent of the nation's endowment and 66 percent of its financial assets. Whereas the son of a peasant customarily received his inheritance—whether a plot of land or a bundle of cash—at age thirty, at present legacies are received around age sixty. The entire mechanism of patrimonial transmission is jammed by a stretching out of the initial sequence, without counting the legitimate forms of exasperation which such postponements of enjoyment provoke among the entitled. Those who have don't redistribute and those who don't have diminish the sums to be redistributed. Those living off their capital, who are all too well provided for, propel the cost of real estate beyond reasonable levels in our city-centers (which are engorged with women and men made anxious by their inability to drive a car or climb a flight of stairs, and frequently condemned to isolation and distance from treatment centers), thus contributing to the penury of affordably priced housing. The insolvent, benefiting from excessive assistance, contribute to the increase in obligatory exactions, which in turn proves fatal to the morale of households. A speedier rotation of consumers would replace that downward spiral with a chain reaction more propitious to a retriggering of growth. It has been calculated that a single point less (or better) in the increase of the aged, inactive sector of the population would lead to a decrease of .9 percent in the rate of obligatory taxation, including the overseas departments, with an accumulated surplus of 6.7 percent over a period of five years. The decrease in income tax would thus cease being a perpetual promise and become a current benefit, with the government in a position to point to that accomplishment assured of its reelection.

I shall not impute the catastrophes of longevity to the progress of medicine alone, a maneuver that would be as simplistic as explaining the declining birth rate by contraception. If one can not hold the social services, with their triumphs over venereal diseases and tuberculosis, to be without blame nor exonerate the campaigns against tobacco and alcohol of all responsibility, many other variables need to be taken into account. If septuagenarian competence is at present better than twenty years ago, and if no openings are to be found in the ever-green programs of our universities (or in our golf clubs, cruises and rotary clubs), it is not due merely to the fact that illnesses are being better treated, but also to nourishment, widespread refrigeration, vacations, antibiotics, recreational walking, individual bedrooms, and levels of education. The risks of survival—insurance companies are paid for such knowledge—are not calculated according to simple models, and it is not by accident that geriatrics is the medicine of complexity. And even if there are grounds for fearing that therapeutic cloning will issue in a new leap in life expectancy at birth, and thus in an insatiable demand for treatment and a downsizing of businesses under pressure of American-style pension funds, no one can or should impede the free advance of biotechnological research. The future, in this respect, has nothing very glorious about it. All of which is another reason, independent of any electoral demagoguery, for the powers that be to confront long-term considerations, focusing their efforts on the elastic variable, which alone offers a margin for maneuver: namely, average life expectancy in our societies. This entails working oneself free of the ideas of the past and eliminating bottlenecks. Or even a new war of the sexes with reverse odds: centenarian males are still eight times less numerous than females.

In a democracy it is impractical to call on the productive half of the population to take responsibility for the physical well-being of the other half. It would be unrealistic to require those starting out in life to feed, cleanse, clothe, and attend to those who have made a point of staying on (even as they complain of being stuck in their plight). And it would be just as illusory, given the situation of the CAC 40 stock index, to pretend to professionalize the administration of decrepitude. Common sense and budgetary constraints forbid the endless proliferation of specialized personnel (physicians, nurses, health auxiliaries, etc.) while extending the endless machinery of deferred extinction (the painful succession of tests, medical exams, treatments, diets, hospitalizations, and interventions to which the non-readaptable are subjected). In the near future it will fall to the state as guarantor of the common good to compensate with structural adjustments for the *hubris* of a medical Prometheus gradually degenerating into the exorbitant Faust who, in violating the timeless wisdom of nature, imperils the future of our economic system and a national solidarity that has at last achieved viability. The stakes are high. The value-added tax of the local merchant or the compensation offered to the Languedoc grape-grower after a hailstorm must not be our model. The question of old age, in which we would do well to distinguish between the secondary and the essential, compassion and management, will depend on the future, on a model of society which is the honor of the West. Any retreat would be tantamount to defeat. However meritorious, the administration of our ills is no longer adequate. It cannot be denied that a serious effort was made on the occasion of a random heat wave (August 2003):

fifteen thousand deaths in two weeks—five times more than the World Trade Center in 2001 and ten times more than the Terror of 1793—is not negligible, but we should not overlook the fact that those excess deaths, affecting persons already in a precarious state, would in any event have ensued over the course of the following year. A demographic recovery should not be dependent on weather-related accidents, meteorology being too imprecise a science, and the coincidence of two sacrosanct principles—the house arrest of the toothless and the non-negotiable aspect of the month of August for families—is not necessarily to be expected in the near future. Global warming is a slow phenomenon, and serious heat waves, with drought, dysentery, and, in the recent past, rioting or famines, etc., intervene only once or twice per century (1719, 1859, 1968, 1994). Exceptional winters may also be of service in the future. But we should not let our imaginations get the better of us: preventive measures baptized in France "Plan Heat Wave"—a sunhat for the indigent, a portable atomizer for each intern in a retirement home, and one fan per cell in houses of confinement—will not significantly improve the submortality rate. It is common knowledge that the heat wave of 2003 ultimately benefited not demographers, but physicians and air-conditioning salesmen.

The disencumbering in the short term of hospitals and hospices, and, in the longer term, the smoothing out of an age-distribution pyramid distorted by gaps and bulges, become totally dysfunctional, will require a combination of discipline and education. It will be imperative to communicate all the more effectively, but without the customary bureaucratic pieties. For in our climes, the tendency is to put off wrinkling later and later, and to do so in terms that are increasingly euphemistic; while the social services, which are going bankrupt with their palliative provisions, gloss over such incoherence by sweetening their nomenclature. One no longer says the Ancients or "our elders," all of which smacks too much of the regiment, the rural sub-prefecture, and the prize-distribution ceremonies of 1880. Nor even "veterans," such reminders being taken out of mothballs only once or twice a year, for November 11 or Omaha Beach. Our hypocrisy produced a feeble "third age" around 1950, at about the same time as the optimistic "third world," that phantom third-estate at present facing ruin. Currently "seniority" is the preferred euphemism for decrepitude. *Senior citizen*, in France, is to "old fart" what *audially challenged* is to stone deaf and *surface technician* is to street-cleaner: an onerous concession. Think of all that the French railroads lose on their "senior citizen cards." And it is not the public services alone that are affected.... Seniors do not spare the streets any more than the rails. It is to such hobbling silhouettes, leashed to quadrupeds relieving themselves of their costly loads, that we are beholden for our sidewalks pocked with excrement, forcing even the most straightforward among us to zigzag their way down the street. One dreams of a general end to pollution of the public thoroughfare, to be sure, but in the interim, we have to *pay*: tens of millions of euros annually for the city of Paris alone, as may be ascertained by checking one's local taxes.

Whatever remains of *virtue* in our spoiled souls— in the republican sense of the word, to wit "the continual preference of the public interest over one's own"—can not but rebel at such equivocation. We all have the obscure sense that in the book of life, the final decorative flourish and the actual end rarely coincide. Our most advanced city-planners envisage necropolises of five hundred thousand places in underground parking lots; we cleanse the surface of our cities of every hint of death, and our physicians outdo themselves, in their oxygen tents, in prolonging comas and delaying the end. We cut corners on funeral expenses and go all out when it comes to intensive care. We no longer tolerate funeral processions, which slow down traffic, but subsidize decrepitude, prolong suffering, and cram every available hospice. Nothing for the dead, everything for the dying. Are we not being incoherent? Why so content with the biodegradable *post* and so obsessed with the biodegrading *ante*.

*   *   *

Whether in the past for families and the sisters of charity, or currently for the state and territorial collectivities, "the unfortunates deserving of our compassion" have always been a charge. What is new is that they have now become an obscenity. The fact may be regretted, but not ignored. Individuals said to be "at risk" are so above all for the prospering of our values, our well-being, and our good humor. It is painfully obvious that a biped without strong desires, barely inclined, despite all the inducements of advertising, to move about, shop, and communicate, no longer has a place in an emulation-based society dedicated to mobility, consumption, and communication. We are intent on constructing our identities freely, with a polychrome flair and a taste for the hybrid: the peeling and fissured surface bespeaks an affiliation to which we submit, a glitch in identity and the reemergence of the dust from which we emerge. Our agenda is autonomy: an individual out of phase is dependent in eating, getting around, or defecating. In the face of speed and the advantages of rapid reaction, he is slow and lethargic. Of nomadic mobility, changing one's décor, he is sedentary, has lead in his ass. As for pleasure, he doesn't give any. Muscles? Doesn't have any. Beauty? Awful. Speaking of grandpa as some sort of bottleneck jammed with deficits is nonetheless a form of politeness. In so doing one neutralizes his destabilizing force by characterizing the dilapidated as merely useless, a dead weight or a burden. It is in fact a factor of physical insecurity and psychic depression for whoever would pretend to be the legislator of his own life. That anti-value, that quivering but stubborn negation of our every long-term plan, as far as we who have embraced our age are concerned, violates our rights and principles, and the mere hint of it can instill in the most active of us a pernicious nihilism. The "there's nothing left of us," which serves as a leitmotiv for the aged whom we visit on the run— and who cannot all be reduced, so much for stereotypes, to carping, penny-pinching invalids—tends to be translated by the compassionate souls we claim to be as a "yes, it's frightful, for us, they represent anything. We should make a greater effort." All this is vapid sentimentality: they are no longer worth anything intrinsically, in general, and in the absolute. Even if we are of a "certain age," we all retain a vital need to grasp the future as a realm of accomplishment, and it is an aggression to exhibit, instead, a varicose vein, or an arthritic limb. Life as a crescendo is the democratic promise. The out-of-phase and out-of-money, hobbling insidiously in our direction, glance at us out of the corner of their eyes, with a nasty undercurrent of: "No need to rush; you'll never make it." Indeed, the mere sight of one of the infirm, revealing the untenable promise, diffidently trumpeting the triumph of our biological program over every and any political agenda, is a live grenade casually tossed on the path of our collective well-being. A cowardly attack against modernity at its most exalting: the perspective of a society in full bloom, bereft of petty dramas and conflicts, reconciled with itself, in which everyone's sneakers fit perfectly. Caution, which is as valid a principle when it comes to muscle tone as for rivers and fields, should physically protect, to the extent possible, society's winners from it.

It was not always thus. Every epoch has the preferred age it deserves, and our devotion to youth would have dumbfounded our predecessors.

The dismissal of the exiting guard by the guard relieving it is plainly linked, as the jargon has it, to the replacement of "past-oriented" societies by others that are "future-oriented," a process which reverses the direction of time's arrow. Over a period of two millennia, growing old was tantamount to acquiring value. Until the Renaissance, the more a doctrine, religion, dynasty, law, custom, or secret could claim to be ancient, the more it was deemed to be worthy of trust, and a vehicle of truth. In order to endow a myth with credibility and render it respectable, the Greeks declared it to be Egyptian; the Romans, Greek; and the medieval lords, Roman. Among those exiled from the golden age of their choice, progress was made by catching the previous day's train. The deck has been reshuffled, and with the turbulent invasion of Progress, the Quarrel of the Ancients and the Moderns, faith in the vanguard, and *le dernier cri*, the Ancestor, who had served for centuries as a guarantor for his junior, a certificate of worthy provenance, and a label of quality, has become his foil. The signature on a counterfeit. To be avoided at any cost. The gerontocratic mold, which was broken during the Renaissance, enjoys a posthumous existence of sorts, through thick and through thin, in the organization of our religions, whether revealed or not, in which the faithful remain convinced of an infinite debt toward the founders, icons, and relics, which have articulated the Norm and the Law, once and for all. Ever since the Academies surrendered to the media, they have become the last precincts, along with the lodges of Freemasonry, in which the applicant can be more or less sure that the hierarch will not be an incarnation of youth but a Venerable. As may be seen in the case of mosques bereft of a permanent imam. Assembled Muslims will spontaneously choose as their leader in prayer the oldest among them, who may not be the most competent, but will be the wisest. This too can die. The Jews, who would be the people of memory and seniority par excellence, have just rebaptized the Old Testament the "First Testament." For them too freshness seems to be the new criterion. Tradition is never betrayed more skillfully than by its own adepts.

There is no age for being old, according to common sense. This is a lie. Ours is undoubtedly the least suited to run that risk and convince others to run it. It is the first in which "one should always feel young." Old age has a history, which is more or less constant from the Middle Ages to the eighteenth century, when it undergoes a rebound with the invention of eye-glasses. Childhood, which is an invention, and a rather late one at that, of the communal school, has a history as well. As does youth, which became an age unto itself, with obligatory military service, and which television, motorcycles, and recorded music have recently granted a rather robust second wind. Old age, on the other hand, despite facelifts, creams, ointments, and organized tours, is currently suffering its worst period in our climes. In comparison, Molière's enthralled graybeard, Georges de La Tour's "aged fortune teller," or Goya's grimacing sorceresses enjoy a certain sovereignty. A very strange reversal indeed: it is when the 65-100 age group in Europe has attained its highest social and physical plateau—by winning the demographical battle, and occasionally the battle of appearances—that its moral authority plummets to its lowest. It is when old age can no longer be stopped, that one can no longer bear to look at it in paintings.

This misfortune can be explained. It has never been easy to be the contemporary of one's own epoch. We would fail to understand our own if we did not take into account four objective factors which demand of our political leaders a change of perspective, whether out of nobility of feeling or not.

1. *The passage from a transmission-based society, in which time is the crucial dimension, to a society based on immediate communication, in which*

space prevails. The accelerated renewal of the sciences as well as the precipitousness of our technological generations have as their result that there is precious little left to transmit from upstream down. The wheel of human generations has begun to turn in reverse. For the Inuit teenager in his Nikes, plugged into his video-games, grandpa the seal-hunter is useless, from another planet. The adolescent with his various prostheses no longer has any need to hunt on an ice floe in order to nourish himself and illuminate his surroundings. Light butter from the supermarket, transported by plane, costs less. There are generation gaps in every generation, but the current one is unlike any in the past: it is not existential, but onto- and technological. It is not so much that we reject the rancid and the old-hat, fighting free of the law of the fathers, reducing the decrepitude of morality and tradition to tabula rasa. It is that with our screens, keyboards, and mouses, there is no longer anything appetizing on grandpa's table. Ours is the first civilization in which acquired competence has become an obstacle for the competence we wish to acquire; in which the young can figure things out better than their seniors; where the younger are more knowledgeable and expert than their elders, who discreetly peer over the shoulders of their children in order to find out how the latest software works. Exit the old man of law, study, and science, with his old-fashioned garb, cap on his head, before his lectern at the fireside, with his in-folios and his astrolabes. He who inspired respect provokes derision—and for good reason. The bearer of the pass-words between the dead and the living currently finds himself the victim of a technological layoff.

2. *The transition from a work-based culture to a leisure-based culture.* We learn how to work; we do not learn how to have fun. There are no longer secrets or tricks of craft to be received from a master in the way in which the aspiring cabinet-maker, locksmith, or plasterer did in times past. The long apprenticeships of the Tours de France, with their stages and certificates of advancement, no longer serve any purpose in an age when it is enough to pay in order to be amused. One swipes one's card and turns the dial. Our civilization of the least possible effort for the most gratification can well do without torch-bearers, with the exception of "Son et Lumière" light shows or the Olympics, for decorative effect. Team sports mobilize national pride, an outlet for suspect energies dammed up by peace and its various discretions: the aged are not party to those indispensable celebrations, neither players nor fans nor vandals.

The exhibition of young, healthy bodies, skilled and profitable, does not have the naiveté of a propaganda gimmick, one *more* gimmick, as during the time of Pétain, with its jamborees and torch-lit retreats. It is an economic necessity, indispensable for the successful functioning of our cultural and celebratory industries. It is no longer a matter of making heads turn on Sundays, but the machine itself, every day of the week. The "national revolution" of 1940, and its boy-scout-inspired insipidity, its calls to European youth, its predilection for camp fires, arched torsos and short pants, were on the order of an incantation. We are infinitely more consistent since only a cash-based liberation of individuals can bestow on the young their role as central stimulus.

3. *The transition from a hope-based era to an era of impatience*. The old are delectable to whoever is capable of taking his time. What is fully ripened is to be savored. We, on the other hand, swallow in a single gulp. We no longer have any confidence in tomorrow, that is: posterity; we demand stories that are short, villas rented by the week, not the month; we call plenitude the instantaneous revelation of the self, and freedom the capacity to reinvent ourselves anew on a daily basis, explosively.

The consecration of the instant, days lived on an emergency footing, newsflashes, the patience of destinies sacrificed to the haste of careers do not merely render the individual who disposes of his time and has little to do unbearable to the restless adept of the high-speed train, the addict of his own appointment book, who no longer has time to do anything (in as much as the former never stops harassing the latter with written requests, pleas for meetings or interventions, altogether boring visits, etc.). An omnipresent nervousness has replaced the seven-year term with one of five at the head of the French state. Painting, a painful apprenticeship, has been supplanted by photography in our chic galleries, and we have all but thrown out of court that art of waiting for a death—of an old aunt, or a great-uncle—which so fascinated Balzac at a time when young people of good family still had hopes, and thus bouquets of flowers in hand, smiles, and Mother's Days. When the slightest delay exasperates us, once the execution of reduced rights of succession has been completed, we kick impatiently against our restraints. The scion's perception of the two-legged moneybox is in no need of strategy. We want everything and we want it right away. This somewhat crude "presentism" has notably perturbed the sweetness of the family nest, and everyone still has ringing in his ears *sotto voce* conversations around the Sunday table, during inexorable and abominable family lunches ("Where in the world did you hide the key to the safe at the back of the entrance closet?" "Tell me, is it so difficult for you to wait a little, as I myself did when I was your age, with Nanny and Jules?") Much like the surreptitious glances of the grandson at the handle of the fish-knife (Genuine silver or silver-plated? Square blade, awkward to use, or like the profile of helmeted Minerva, a felicitous sign?). Let us not insist. The environment is unhealthy. With the laws on inheritance establishing fixed portions for direct descendants (the others being subject to such exorbitant taxes that it may ultimately be preferable not to figure in a will), it becomes evident to those juniors who retain a sense of family that given the number of sufferers from Alzheimer's, one is engaged in a losing struggle. The acquired habit of an equitably calculated exchange of services (be they monetary or not) will induce the mature to invest in the young. "At least," one tells oneself, "when I knit a sweater for the little monster or take him to the movies to see an unbearably vulgar trifle," while stroking my ungainly beard, "he will remember later on, there will be a recompense, it will not be time wasted."

4. *Transition from the graphosphere to the videosphere.* It is an observable fact: where age is honored, images pay the price. Where the interplay of images erodes the weight of words, it means bad times for our seniors. The narcissism of photos, television, and movies is more matter of fact than that of print: it demands irreproachable shapes and smooth skins (with or without Photoshop).

The assistance policies intended to turn our walking ruins into men like any others, and rotting humanity into silver-haired senior citizens (aware, but independent and gleeful), the various modes of administering the "third age," that *allegro ma non troppo* of life's course, were all put in place in France right after the war, before the advent of the videosphere. That regimen comes with its own cruelty, since what goes unseen is as though it did not exist. Whence the cruel choice of the post-modern oldster: either he is on display and provokes disgust or he isn't and is done away with altogether. Invisible as part of a collective fate, the worn-out subject poses a problem for his fellow creatures on the go solely as a physical specimen, capable only, for his misfortune, of reflecting light rays on a photosensitive surface.

We have learned from the physiologists that our internal organs age rather well. Only the skin—what is deepest in us, according to Valéry—suffers significant damage over time. It is all rather unfortunate: whereas youthfulness of heart and mind is shielded by its inherent modesty, skin is made to be seen and, worse yet, touched. That is the tipping point, the irremediable moment of reversal. At present there are no longer any thoughts without emotions or *frissons*. What must our young dauphins atop their rollerblades, skis, and surfboards, sliding and gliding as smoothly as possible, think of the creviced creatures, the scaly, grainy, chafed hides that come and go before their eyes? Or of the cracked, mottled epidermis shared, at both ends of the social scale, by the red-necked farmer and the jewel-bedecked star, baked in ultraviolet, and no-longer-all-that-young? What moral respect may reasonably be expected on the part of those total-look teens, all smoothness and flow, for those haunted and haggard retards, with their cardiac arrhythmia, silent-film gestures, and leaking tear-ducts? The conflict is no longer at the level of obligation but of sensation—the silken, pearled, and shimmering versus the worn out, creviced, and faded; radiant versus dull; lubricated versus dessicated. The case of the "handsome old gent" will be offered in opposition. And we will not deny having come across a few: Aragon, Agnelli, Clint Eastwood,

42

Jean Daniel.... But how many, enjoying that label, turn out to be aging playboys, with their coquettish poses, matching socks and handkerchief, toupee readjusted and crow's feet "reworked," pathetic counterfeits? As though all one needed were a Stetson to be a Marlboro man. Do a number of former beauties have their skin tightened, breasts lifted, nose straightened? Absolutely, but their hands, overlooked by our septuagenarian Lolitas, remain, and those mottled and crusted extremities, which our plastic surgeons are wrong to ignore, make things all the more obvious: knotted, grainy, with protruding-blue veins amidst spots of yellow. In times past, dowagers handed in their mittens for gloves of a coarser fiber, the better to conceal their iguana-like excrescences. It was a matter of decency, even delicacy. But those were other times.

We should not be surprised to see aging skin banished from TV, excluded from billboards and magazine covers; nor should we hold it against the young that they prefer their screens to their grand-mas. It is a reflex reaction of self-defense. A preventive measure. Deodorized vs. fermented; oxygenated flow vs. oxidized stock; stretchable vs. foldable: in brief, night and day. For by announcing in advance the uselessness of the struggle, those exemplars of collective demobilization, heralds of the final defeat, dining at six o'clock and waking up at four, not only undermine the psychosomatic equilibrium of our vital forces, which they cut off at the knees. They diminish the most intimate core of our being. A handicapped individual does not wound our pride. He is an accident. We may have pity for him, but at no cost. Old age is commonplace. It stretches its arms out to us all. It is to little avail that we learn in school that multicellular organisms are not made to last; out of the kitchen trudges an all too compromising degenerate, whose deficiencies and flaws cannot be attributed to external factors, as one does for poverty, prostitution, or hunger—evil exploiters, rapacious multinational corporations, urban corruption, atmospheric pollution, an accommodating lifestyle, or a lack of physical exercise (one knows of septuagenarian marathoners). Senescence is a form of degeneration that admits of no solution through eugenics, no attempt at regeneration through a methodical de-weeding of the species, no search for a scapegoat. Unless it be life itself as a regulatory system, whose proper functioning rests on all these local catastrophes. The defective stock is none other than ourselves. Ample reason for keeping our distance.

We moderns are born fighters. Gentle commerce has deprived us of enemies, but we still fight on, always and everywhere. Against cancer. Against exclusion. Against unemployment. Against failure in school. Against homophobia, racism, and anti-Semitism. But how are we to fight against the hours and days? Against fate? Against the part of life that does not admit of choice? Our life is and is supposed to remain a Disney theme park, a video game in which broken toys are immediately replaced, the cowboy killed by the Indian gets up, the film is rewound, and the dial turned back to zero with the flick of a finger. The biological clock refuses to play by the rules—in which regard every burial is a form of betrayal. It unwinds in only a single direction. This is the scandal, both nauseating and inherently unfair, which deserves to be banned. The soothing motions of the market will not suffice. Action must be taken. Fate will not have the last word. *No pasarán.*

"It will never happen to me!" Baggy eyes, stringy hair, exaggerated jowls, double chin: save it for the others. The pasty face growing wider every morning than long, imperceptibly, with no cosmetic that does the trick... The young are disturbed at our sight because we have the face *they* deserve, and deep down they know, the buggers, that the day after tomorrow it will be theirs. We pardon them. If we ourselves, at age sixty, cannot in all decency bear the gaze of the grotesque and misshapen twin looking at us each morning from our bathroom mirror... That faithful enemy does not, of course, look like us, no? Let us be brief.... Such is the spirit of the age: we have no wish to see the consequences of our efforts. Whereas the old-style missionary, in 1920, took off for what remained of his life, and the French *coopérant*, in 1960, for two years, the humanitarian worker, in 2000, completes his mission in two months. The first was anonymous; the second, a government employee; the third, a hero. As a shrewd observer of the behavior of the young put it: "We always end up killing, symbolically or physically, whomever we do not accord the right to exist within ourselves and to whom we ultimately refuse the right to exist at all."[*] That outcast, wherever we switch him off, is the laggard.

The number of unclaimed corpses at the end of the month of August 2003, throughout France, speaks for itself: our policies concerning the aged lag behind our reflexes. The timidity of the powers that be on the subject of euthanasia is, at the very least, out of phase. Or beside the point. When it comes to efflorescence without decay, families turn out to know more than the government. Why not admit as much? In that eternal present of sex and

---

[*] Philiipe Meirieu, *L'Ecole ou la guerre civile* (Paris: Plon, 1997), p. 128.

amusement in which we are all, willingly or not, immersed, the dismissal of the negative will be less onerous than believed. We have a phobia of death, and we have taken the necessary measures to remove it from our field of vision and curtail our mourning. We are obsessed with growing old—the latter because of the former—and we do not yet possess the legislation adequate to our aversion. It is an inherently perilous circumstance.

*   *   *

We would run the most serious risks if we were to consign our fate to inertia, which has always placed its bets, quite frivolously, on prolonging things. For our time is limited. Old age, in France, and in Europe, has not yet realized that it exists. That future force, even if it constitutes a relatively unified social category, currently possesses relatively limited bargaining power. For lack of having achieved a clear awareness of itself, the gray continent has not yet delivered itself of the fearsome pressure group it bears within its loins. At present every individual defines himself by gender, origin, sexual orientation, or religion, and is represented by a matching lobby. The 65-100 age bracket, minimally or poorly targeted by our major corporations, has not yet constructed its cultural identity. It has not yet acquired the autonomy of manners and references achieved by European youth of the 1930s, with the Popular Front's *maisons de la jeunesse*, the parades of *Hitlerjugend*, and the proud Romans singing *Giovinezza* at the top of their lungs. In the face of "youth culture" (age 16-24), there is no "age culture." There are certainly remnants of associative life to be found (affinity groups, "senior gatherings," rotary clubs, etc.), but no Movement of the Aged, no Miss Maturity. A great dormant power aspires to senior power. If the young, in all their amorphousness, who might well have been swallowed up by their environment like a blotter, have managed, in spite of everything, to build a separate world for themselves, the old too will not be lacking in motives for marking their territory. Their marshmallow-soft demeanor will not last indefinitely. Is their generational unity lacking in contour? Retirement at 60 or 65 used to be a clear and distinct rite of passage (like the vote at eighteen or the draft for the young). The age of retirement, to be sure, has fluctuated, and the termination of work can at present begin officially with sick leave. Membership may be spreading like an oil slick, but identification is still a bit fluid. In the broader sense eligibility would be open to all those for whom tomorrow will not be a new day, but the same as yesterday, only worse. All those men and women, like you and me, who would do well to answer (should they manage to combine politeness with precision), as Fontenelle replied to Chamfort asking him how "things were going," that they were not "going" at all, they were going away. That would include quite a few, in the broadest sense. It is difficult at present to offer a count or classification for these depleted individuals, who fit into so many categories. Where shall we place him? He is not one of the sick to be treated, which would take him to the hospital. Not a delinquent to be reintegrated, which would point him toward prison. Not one of the handicapped to be rehabilitated, which would send him to a clinic. Not, or not always, a derelict to be tucked away, which would assign him to the police station. That absence of an official pigeonhole and its concomitant reduced social visibility (no specific press) do not, however, allow us to exclude the prospect of a transnational May '68 of those discarded for reason of anachronism. With the young having been normalized, formatted to the hilt, we shall perhaps witness a shift toward the opposite end, the exit of that culture of rejection (of inauthenticity, compromise, mendacity, etc.) which our entrants no longer exemplify. Might that future elite counter James Dean and Brando with Ginger and Fred, hip-hop with the waltz or foxtrot, the motorcycle with the rocking chair, and booming decibels with the silence of the chat room? It is altogether possible, but it should not be forgotten that the preferred musical genre of the aged in France (or at least of those not stuck, during adolescence, in the goo of Tino Rossi, but electrified by Mick Jagger) remains rock. Let us prepare for the day when, with the rebellion of tomorrow's Spartacus subsiding, the Ministry of Youth, National Education, and Sports will ebb into a mere government division for the immature, since serious matters, in our intravenous Venice, will have passed to the Ministry of Old Age, Minimality, and Tombstones. It is not, after all, cradles that are defaced by swastikas....

It is almost as though the situation conferred on the aged by the twentieth century were not without recalling that of women in the nineteenth, once one adds on the right to vote (but to what end?) and drops needlework. The new voiceless, collectively transparent, attend to their petty affairs, in the margins, just as women once did at home. They play at *boules* and poker with the same discreet docility with which mothers used to mend socks, sweep floors, and teach catechism. And the same hypocrisy eases our remorse. Did we once have mothers and whores? We now have patriarchs and old farts. We bless our vegetables the better to let them rot. We worship Victor Hugo, Albert Einstein, Sister Emmanuel, the age 95, in order, once our prayers have been said, to deprive grandpa of his soup or attach him to his bed if he becomes too much of an inconvenience. Just as we used to pray to the Mother of God, Joan of Arc, and Marie Curie the better to rivet our better half to the oven. If only our own strange outsiders might in the future control their mortality, as women their birthrate. In order to do so, devout women once had to emancipate themselves from their parish priests. Our quivering quibblers will have to emancipate themselves from their family doctors in order to seize the right to die with dignity. For the devotees of the medical congregation will one day learn at their expense that their preferred charge is their number-one enemy.

To be sure the inexactitude of the parallel is misleading. What the aged (particularly those without resources) experience as an injustice corresponds rather accurately to their actual value. The female population contributes notably to growth because it procreates first, thus renewing the available capacity for leisure, and works later (both after and before menopause). It is normal that the collectivity should take greater care of the creators of its wealth than of others. Whether we like it or not, "the evolution of the price of human life is an essential component in the calculation of the economic profitability of public investments." A Canadian economist, Fernand Martin of the University of Montreal, assigned by the Ministry of Transportation to determine whether it was profitable to rebuild roads on which serious accidents, costing society millions of dollars, tended to occur; he properly replied that it all depended on the economic value of the individuals whom such projects might eventually save. Now the price of the life of a human being is not calculated in the abstract. The expert in question evaluated it at fifty million euros for the "head of a business and father of a family," and at only thirty million euros for an "inactive senior citizen." Without entering into the details and modalities of the calculation, we can state that the estimate strikes us as rather objective and plausible. Were it more widely known, it would tend to appease a good number of *subjective* resentments.

In the absence of any real public debate on the subject, it is to be feared that a demagogue will some day develop that false analogy—between today's domination by youth and yesterday's by masculinity. One may recall the old banner reading: "One man out of two is a woman." What is to be expected from "One voter out of two is elderly"? Will we witness an Elderly Liberation Movement taking the place of a Women's Liberation Movement already fatigued by its victories? Chronicles of "ordinary agism" after those of ordinary sexism, violence against persons and property compensating for the violating of bodies? There are more elderly assaulted, after all, than women. If we have succeeded in stigmatizing offenses to the dignity and image of women in daily life, one can only imagine the number of recriminations issuing from a League for the Rights of the Elderly. Every day of the week they are insulted, derided, aggressed, humiliated, harassed, and stigmatized because they have a cane, white hair, dentures, a hearing aid, or a prostate. Yet every political party has a Commission on Culture, Education and Youth, and not a single one has a Commission on Boredom, Solitude, and Old Age. Legislators and our highest authorities do endless battle against all forms of discrimination, whether they stem from racism, religious intolerance, sexism, or homophobia, and no one has yet thought of adding "and regarding age." In the face of the ridicule routinely suffered by "old goats," how many Muslims, Jews, and Gypsies would fail to file suit? Anti-racism is the law of the day; anti-agism awaits its turn. When the elderly awaken, Europe will tremble.

In the interim, only the Lord knows how vulnerable our pensioners in fact are. Even without evoking the horrors hidden away in certain licensed retirement homes, of which we are occasionally informed in police reports, generally on page 13, in the lower left-hand corner.

Public health. Ask anyone: what is the urgent issue?, and he will reply: HIV. The gay lobby has its genius, and it is a scandal that nine sufferers out of ten in the world do not have access to care. But in our countries, this is an illusion. AIDS kills around five hundred people a year in France, Alzheimer's eighty thousand. More than a hundred times as many. It is the third highest cause of mortality, after cancer and cardio-vascular disease. Estimates of HIV-carriers run to 120,000, but Alzheimer patients over age seventy number 850,000 (with a hundred thousand new cases each year). An "Alzheimer agenda" was adopted in 2001. Concrete measures and their funding have yet to be implemented. The program envisaged seven thousand new entry slots each day. Barely half have been obtained, and in ten years there will be two million victims in our country. The airwaves and budgets go to AIDS sufferers. Make way for the young!

Go to a hospital. You're seventy years old? You will be placed at the end of the corridor. Staff will enter your room without knocking. You will be treated with unwanted familiarity. Do you need a scanner, a relatively rare and costly device? Come back in a month; it is reserved on a priority basis for patients under sixty. With the oldest patients, those treated least well, everything is done with an eye to economy. The measures recently trumpeted with great fanfare are, to be sure, intended to create health-sector jobs for the untrained ("life auxiliaries," without degrees) in order to lower the unemployment rate. The young handicapped individual has access to aides eligible for certain forms of compensation; not so the elderly, who are obliged to pay for their means of transportation. Interns know that only recently such and such an elderly hospitalized patient was not deemed to be worth a visit from the supervisor in his daily rounds. (Fracture of the femoral neck? We can skip it.) Geriatrics remains a marginal specialty, distinctly secondary and an object of scorn—without technical innovation. Few academic promotions. Sixty beds in all of Paris.

Consider the ads on TV. "Elderly individuals" make it to the screen only on condition that they play at being young. Grandma is expected to bite into her candy while looking like an ecstatic child, and grandpa to win a set of tennis in order to sell a shirt. Soon they will make him imitate a spinning top, his baseball cap on backwards, as rap requires.

An old person on display does not have the right to be old. Act young and shut up. Our elderly have so well assimilated that sense of shame that they will turn any anti-wrinkle cream into a success. And that brings us back to our point. Walk into a drugstore and head to the cosmetics shelf. The anti-wrinkle cream, with identical molecules, sells for twice the price of anti-acne cream. Let the elderly pay. Make room for the young!

Go to your local newsstand, or to your web server. Is there a magazine, radio station, or TV network in the hands of a contingent of seniors? The mass media are alleged to be ruled by quantitative considerations. The younger-than-twenty bracket is less numerous in France than those over fifty-five, but seniors, who are voracious readers of news, have only the right to consume in this domain, not to produce. The invisible ones are expected to look on at the Gay Pride parade in silence and lower their eyes—there will never be a parade for the unsightly. Five hundred thousand gays armed with microphones and cameras inspire our lawmakers to take a stand. Thirteen million voters over age sixty, without access to parade routes and the air waves, are reduced to hiding in doorways. Beauty, truth, and goodness are currently determined by Inrocks and Technikart. Have you ever heard anyone, in a review of magazine journalism, mention *Pleine Vie* or *Notre Temps*, honorable Catholic publications devoted to the "third age," which sell ten times as many copies and exert ten times less influence? The very young have so perfected the art of self-infatuation that they are no longer able to take an interest in anyone else. In sum: an over-representation of some, who are different, in the minority, but legitimate, and un under-representation of others, who are different, in the majority, but uncool. Make room for difference, as long as it's young!

Go to a bookstore. There are an infinite number of works by sociologists, political scientists, philosophers, etc., on the transformations of cyber-space, the metamorphoses of the future, pre-, post-, and hypermodernity, the access society, man in his computerized, symbiotic, and virtual incarnations. There are admirable investigations, breathtaking prognostications, laser-like observations. You will not find among them the slightest allusion to the place and role of the elderly within the great stampede of the brutes. The man of the future will be young or he will not be. And above all don't open up your newspaper to find out what is going on in the sanitation, education, and judicial sectors, or in the Ministry of Employment and Social Cohesion. Our successive and repetitive "programs to combat exclusion" either circumvent or neglect the non-persons who burden us. The old are fatiguing. Make room for adolescents and for the disadvantaged *young*!

Listen to conversations. To be young is honorific; old, pejorative. How to humiliate a young person? By treating him as old. How to flatter one of the elderly? "You look so young!" *Juvénile*, in French at least, has none of the negativity of *sénile*.... Do you want to discourage interest in (and subsidies for) a religious community: "They're a bit old, don't you think?" Should a presidential candidate want to disqualify his rival, he will suddenly discover him to be "aging" a bit. Aside from the fact that one is hard put to see how anyone, even a politician, might avoid aging (unless by outright suicide), no one, and least of all the guilty party, is given to understand that, "as he ages, the individual grows in wisdom and capacity for synthesis. He brings a certain elevation and perspective to matters. We juniors better watch it. With a dinosaur like that, things are going to start moving." There are compliments that pass unperceived.

Such jeers and grimaces are experienced with a certain pain by those unaware of the objective economic reasons underlying them. Police aides do their best to respond to complaints, but how is one to curb the first impulse of the average civilian, inclined as he is to encourage those who feel they have been abandoned on the side of the road to leave home as infrequently as possible? Collect the confessions of stressed-out "little old ladies"—women seem to accumulate handicaps—upon returning from their errands in the neighborhood. "It's too painful. They treat us like dogs in the bank and the post office. They send us to the Internet for the slightest transaction, and I haven't a clue what to do with their machines. And I'm not even talking about the delinquents that keep on staring at my purse. In any event, they've abandoned us. We are no longer of interest to anyone." One such woman (whom I questioned in the course of this investigation) even added: "I've done my time. This world is no longer mine. I want to leave." "Things are not going well" has always been the refrain of those leaving the scene, in every era. This is no doubt the first in which the leitmotif of the distressed has become: "We disgust people. We are no longer of any use. There is no longer any place for us. Let's declare the show over."

To those who would accuse us of darkening the picture, we would answer with a revealing figure: in ten years, from 1990 to 2000, the consumption of antidepressants in Europe has doubled. In 2003, Europe became third in consumption of pharmaceutical products. Is it at all surprising that 50 percent of the elderly living in institutions and 25 percent of those living at home were acknowledged to be prone to depression?

Put more crudely: things may explode at any moment; there is no time to be lost.

II.

THE SOLUTION?

It is clear that the question of old age, a fateful legacy, will not find an adequate solution within conventional frameworks and notions. It is therefore incumbent on us to leap beyond the failed efforts of the day and offer the outline, however skeletal, of what might constitute an ideal solution. While being aware that today's utopia, as always, will be tomorrow's reality. Even if the querulous, when confronted with our proposal—which is nothing less than a republic within the Republic—would replace the noble word utopia with the pedantic and repugnant term "dystopia," with its suggestion of phantasmagoria and misfortune.

Until now, recommendations evincing "concern for the end of life" have been parliamentary: consensual, but not professional. Generous and vague.

And all the better received, such is the rule, in that they are barely operational. The commission charged by the President of the Assemblée with squaring the circle proposes in its report titled "Respect Life, But Accept Death" to modify marginally several articles of the (penal, public health, and medical) codes currently in force in order to put a damper on therapeutic zeal—without simultaneously legalizing the exception of euthanasia. Such piecemeal measures manage to confirm the *détente* on dying without actually emerging from the pathetic pettiness of the plan for heat waves. Half-measures, incompatible with a clear and strong-willed policy. The key to the problem is not a matter of codes, but of modes, that is, primarily, of establishing a circumscribed sphere of intervention. Drastic situations demand drastic measures.

The greatest ill, in the current case, is human loneliness due to the dispersion of patients and the costly scattering of treatment centers, a circumstance, moreover, which is conducive to mistreatment by particularly impulsive caretakers and refractory to supervision by the appropriate agencies. A first remedy: regrouping of the affected population. Not in a hospital super-complex, nor even in a quarantine-city, but in their own territory. Outside of our urban centers (hospices tend to be *extra-muros*), and not in our suburbs (of the Ivry-sur-Seine variety). What is called for is something bucolic.

Which would provide two advantages: for the Administration, a formidable economizing of resources at every level: training of health care providers (which involve difficult professions, perpetually confronted with the risk of burn-out), mutual oversight, integration of technical services (radiology, anesthesia, surgery, cremation), coordinated execution of protocols. Superior supervision, optimally pursued. Is it rational for a physician to traipse through the countryside to verify the arterial pressure of a mildly diabetic ninety-year old? Or for the mere checking of the prostate specific antigen level of an individual to mobilize a great specialist? Think of the lack of funds of the regional "social and sanitary affairs" administrations of French departments and the shortage of hospital staff (notably the traditional coiffed volunteers, a regrettable effect of de-Christianization), which prevents expert physicians from concentrating on their own work. For the chronically ill at the end of their life, and particularly for the immense sub-category of the aged and insolvent, such large-scale concentration would put a damper on class jealousies (which tend to reemerge with age) and above all would ensure better protection for all, while eliminating the commonplace humiliations associated with the excesses of the youth cult. ("Hey, old-timer, would you mind moving it a little?"). Old age ceases to be a socially onerous condition as soon as there are no suburban trains or public means of transport to take or youngsters to insult it (aside from the service staff). Better yet, in order to eliminate tedium, a classic factor in depression, a large array of productive activities will be reserved for the aged (a bit as is the case in Benedictine and Franciscan establishments). The dereliction of the elderly individual has in fact much to do with his exclusion from the circuit of production (let us not underestimate the pleasures of removing peas from their pod at the back of the garden), a problem which this withdrawal, which is not a retirement, may alleviate in a cost-efficient manner. Safety, good will, and proximity all end up reinforcing each other.

The autonomous turf we are laying claim to here, at once festive and functional, exclusively devoted to the prophylactic organization of many a "happy end," should be able to receive a million individuals each year on a rotating basis (as a function of results obtained). It would be endowed with legal status: which would amount to that rotation itself, as it functions within a clear and even scientifically informed juridical framework. Who would be the beneficiaries of this exceptional offer? It would fall to an independent regulatory agency (with an office in each French department), appointed by the Minister of Public Health, in concertation with the National Order of Physicians, but shielded from the customary pressures of the guild. That watch committee would have as its mission the identification, beyond cases of serious or incurable illness, of the least solvent and/or most fragile subjects among the aged, and to invite them to agree to relocate. The organized evolution from a *transitive* medicine to a *palliative* medicine, intended to facilitate final deliverance, in a manner both painless and respectful of the dignity of individuals, should allow for a gradual rollback of the average age of the male population to around seventy, and the female to seventy-five. A diminution of one point every five years, in particular thanks to the "compassion program"—that statistical and duly verified norm (the low water mark at present being five hundred fifty deaths annually in metropolitan France) would be such, it would appear, as to motivate care-taking personnel in a sector of the work force in which the inability to make future projections is a source of demoralization. The aim of the penitentiary system is *reinsertion*; that of the medical system is *cure*—but until now the hospice and retirement home establishment has had no positive aim, no strategic vision of its role in society. With the new demand for results, and a corresponding system of bonuses, one would have done away, to the satisfaction of all, with that bane of the profession: the absence of any sense of purpose.

The new coherence in methods of intervention, accompanied by prediction-based planning, will not fail to provoke a variety of expected objections on the part of humdrum minds. There will be talk of apartheid, ghettos, suspect biopolitical measures, and even authoritarian eugenics and a consumerist massacre. The sadly renowned battle cry of "kill off the old and enjoy!" will be invoked. But by whom? Most probably by psychiatrists or psychoanalysts, the very individuals who refuse to take charge of "the self-centered do-nothings" or "Auntie Danielles" ("give us a break with your old-timers; we already have the crazies, we don't need the poor"). Our self-regarding, moralizing souls refuse to sully their hands with overnight diapers for the incontinent, glasses to be groped for under formica-topped dressers, and dentures to be cleaned twice daily. Is not medically assisted death, after all, the natural counterpart to medically assisted procreation? If it is indeed the case that from our perspective a man's duties toward his fellow creatures imply a solidarity that is both horizontal (not inconveniencing one's neighbors) and vertical (permitting one's descendents to flourish as optimally and as rapidly as possible), is there any need to specify that the inflection we are proposing (accepting life, but respecting death) has nothing to do with such abject projects as human stables or programs for the elimination of the abnormal, the Apaches, or the prematurely born that have dishonored the history of Europe? We are no where near forgetting the "gentle extermination" of forty thousand of the mentally ill during the Second World War, to the shame of the French medical profession. But the democratic alleviation of suffering, the reduction of waste, and the reinvigoration of growth, even if they entail the computerization of health records, is not the same as the creation of a race of supermen or the fabrication of no-fault elites. It is a matter, once again, not of greater beauty, but of greater profitability and productivity.

It would be inadmissible for an advanced liberal society, as well educated and endowed as our own, which, moreover, is capable of mastering physical pain (the consumption of morphine having happily increased five-fold in the last five years), not to behave any better toward its Ancients than those nomadic and impoverished populations in which elder sons would escort their fathers, when the time came, into the middle of the Sahara or deep into the Amazonian jungle, leaving them to their fate. And do our own families, taking off for vacation, do anything different when they abandon grandma in her attic, with a bottle of water and three crackers? Is it really claimed that house arrest, without any material assistance or psychological support, or forced institutionalization, with tranquillizers and eventually thefts, gags, and deprivation of dinner are better than the establishment of a distinct territory in which the stateless souls of the planet Youth will no longer be clandestine passengers on the trip, but full-blown tourists, supervised by the Social Services Administration, with all the ethical safeguards required? This convivial community, blessed by its landscape, somewhere between a wildlife reserve and a theme park, in which meals will no longer be delivered to individual homes, because one will be free to lunch with one's friends, will have nothing of the elephant graveyard about it, and even less of Victor Hugo's Court of Miracles. Nor will it be a "memory garden" writ large. It will be the "gate to the New World," in which every former child will be able to rediscover Davy Crockett and Central Plaza. And thus will an entire people in its diaspora, which is not even aware of its existence as a people, be endowed with its welcome center, supranational homeland, and—why not?—one day, its own mini-state, with its special passport, police, and courts of law.

Its name? Bioland. At its border checkpoints, there will be only signs reading: Welcome to the Bio Age!

*   *   *

The city, which is artificiality, removes us from the essential, which is biological. It is only immersion in nature, participation in farmwork—raising animals, harvesting, shepherding—which can restore to the city-dwellers of the West, prisoners of their glass and steel cages, the lost sense of the whole which Hindus and Buddhists have so success-fully preserved. Death and rebirth... To live and die in the country, leaving the realm of the brutes for the roundness of days and the circle of seasons, the world of the gods! Reopening the immemorial Book of wisdom, written every evening, with a stroke of the quill, by birds hidden among the foliage when they can no longer fly, horses reclining on the hay when they are no longer able to trot... The choice of a rural setting, serene but not abandoned, not all that inaccessible, but at a certain elevation (if the rich ventilate their elderly, the less favored are rarely kept cool in summer) strikes us as indispensable in facilitating the mental reintegration of the aged into the great cosmic rhythms, the unquenchable and pacifying harmony of the gospel's "If it die...." After a careful study of the different possible zones of implantation and competitive bidding by the regions, the Ardèche strikes us as the best choice to shelter our future Bioland, which will undoubtedly serve as a model in Europe. More specifically we are thinking of the crystalline and turbulent Haut-Vivarais, in the northern sector of the department, bordering on the Forez (to which may be added, in the event of congestion, the beautiful volcanic plane of Coiron, which is bordered by the river that gives its name to the department.) An elevated sense of humanitarian obligation is fitting for exalted lands rich in memory. It would reinitiate old projects (which have, in fact, always remained vague) of "revitalizing the rural environment" through a series of retirement colonies, surrounded by retiree resident farmers engaged in whole earth bio-farming methods and traditional cattle herding. Several members of the General Council, upon consultation, as well as the offices of the Prefecture, have communicated to us their enthusiasm.

The influx of public and private funds needed for planning and setting up the territory, providing adequate residential units and plumbing, the assembling, on the outskirts of the community, of legal personnel, coaches, insurance agents, statisticians, and telecommunications services would clearly constitute a formidable breath of fresh air for a region that has been all but disinherited and is only rarely visited by tourist buses and Mozart festivals.

Beyond its geographical centrality and the remaining thermal waters, which are insufficiently appreciated, several positive factors argue in favor of this choice:

-Considerable annual extremes of temperature, with heat waves in the summer and cold waves in the winter, a circumstance to which enfeebled organisms are not insensitive.

-A rather violent landscape, poor soil quality, the harshness of rural life, combined with extremely abrupt shifts in altitude (occasionally a thousand five hundred meters in the course of thirty or forty kilometers), a situation that cannot be without consequence, over time, for heart patients and asthmatics.

-Sports and relaxation facilities such as horseback riding in the forest, white water kayaking, mountain trails with cliffs and precipices, of a sort to tempt the most courageous individuals.

-The limited number of access routes by land to these green solitudes and the absence of an airport, thus allowing for relatively easy identity checks at entry and exit points, and, consequently, for accurate statistical records.

-Finally, and above all, a historically-grounded long-term tradition of mysticism. There have been numerous questers for the ideal and elevated sentiments who have, in the past, found refuge with members of the indigenous population, harsh of manner but sensitive of soul and generally disinterested (Camisards, Jansenists, etc.) Ample evidence remains in the form of vestiges of abbeys and charterhouses, a few Catholic chapels and monasteries still functioning, and, of greater pertinence for our purposes, flourishing spiritual communities of Eastern or Jungian inspiration, which have come on the scene only recently.

We are fully aware that the old, who detest the young, appreciate the old even less. Old age exacerbates nastiness; it is the age for settling old scores, and first off, against members of one's family. None of which prevents most such individuals from wanting nothing so much as to die at home—an understandable desire, but which the current housing situation, the break-up of families, and the maximizing of pleasures, make it no longer feasible to indulge. Whence the proliferation of shabby old folks' homes hidden away in our suburbs. There will as a result be resistance to what may appear to be an exile aggravated by promiscuity ("when we're with each other, we're bored stiff"). Which is why Bioland will be the antithesis of the old-style retirement home. There will be a combination of the most exhilarating animation and recycling of the far-eastern sort, so that the blessed can awaken simultaneously to the joys of divinity and the whims of Nature re-enchanted. The aim would be to bridge the gap between the Dalai-Lama and Disneyland, prayer and fun, so that anyone might feel himself to be Harry Potter when he awakens and Lama Zen when he goes to bed. Soft music, flower-adorned walkways, potato-sack races, and castles galore, to be sure. But also evening chats and meditations. Teddy bears, pumpkins, and Bermuda shorts will blend, unadorned, with local color—field mice, violet fairs, chestnuts from the underbrush. The right to die with gaiety—the modern word for happiness—will be a subject of consultation with specialists from the other side of the Atlantic. But without ever conflicting with the schedule of lectures by the spiritual masters who will guide interns to the most esoteric summits of humanity. This terminal university curriculum will give ample place to approved doctrines of the transmigration and reincarnation of souls. Regular courses on Buddhist literature and New Age cosmology given by ascetics arriving from Asia will train the old West in the art of "letting go," to which will be adjoined units in elementary biology (adaptative weakening of organisms, difference between somatic cells destined to disappear and germinal cells reproduced from generation to generation, the imperative of reproductive success, etc.). One out of every four Europeans believes in reincarnation. This is insufficient. No mention will be made of classical Christian theology. It might dispel the felicitous confusion, already indulged by one Christian out of two, between resurrection, which only happens once and is not accorded to all, and reincarnation, which is the lot of every individual (to his great misfortune, the Hindu adds) and without waiting for the Last Judgment. Our social security system in France can expect greater benefit from the Wheel than from the Path, and from the Lotus than from the Cross. With Paradise no longer quite credible and Hell too incompatible with Human Rights—it will be a net gain, for the moral comfort of our populations, even those who have been exposed to the waters of baptism, to keep them at a distance from the clichés of alienating monotheism ("the day of reckoning belongs to God alone"). A graceful and timely liberation from the sufferings and disappointments of existence requires that one bring the final impulses of consumers into phase with the consolatory rhythms of nature. There is the ample panoply of branches of the Buddhist tree, to be sure, but also Marcus Aurelius: "All that suits you suits me, oh Cosmos... When the moment of retirement has come, one must submit like the olive which, upon falling, offers thanks to the branch that bore it."

*   *   *

Our proposal would be but one more vanity of the well-intentioned heart if it were not accompanied by measures of motivation, precaution, and preparation.

Concerning *motivation*: the civic sense being what it is, not to mention human nature, it would be prudent to anticipate an allocation of a thousand euros per family for every oldster who has been sidelined (transportation to Bioland will be free). The authorities in Australia allocate three thousand dollars for every baby born. Such is the "new-born bonus." Its equivalent in the end zone, an "elimination bonus," might end up motivating families that are negligent, overly sensitive, or under pressure to fulfill their duty toward society, even if the process, as a result, is accelerated. The margins for maneuver opened up by the closing of retirement homes and the rationalization of support systems should suffice, at the very least, for the financing of this modest assistance.

Concerning *prevention*: from the outset there will be an exemption from the regrouping measures foreseen in this plan for a certain number of subgroups that persist in their noisiness, are to all appearances superfluous, but continue to contribute, directly or indirectly, to the gross national product. (1) Aged individuals subject to a tax on their wealth (under certain conditions: an annual cruise to the tropics, residence in a five-star hotel in a thermal retreat, subscription to the Paris Opera, charitable contributions to the Friends of the Louvre and the Château of Versailles). (2) Members of the Five Academies of the Institute, plus the Goncourt Academy, as well as certain deserving artists, researchers, and senators, selected on the basis of their record by the National Council for Risk-Prevention. (3) Those decorated by the Légion d'honneur and several other orders of merit (not including the Palmes académiques and the

Order of Agricultural Merit). Since the three afore-mentioned categories have every chance of boiling down to no more than one, we shall add to them (4) religious clergy and ecclesiastics, despite their feeble income, but in homage to the abbé Pierre and in light of the services they continue to render to the collectivity and the decline in religious callings in our seminaries. It would be counter-productive to thin out the already sparse ranks of those charged with officiating at milestone ceremonies (baptisms, weddings, burials).

Concerning *education*: our objective presupposes a national mobilization, with a campaign of radio spot ads targeting the 18-35 age bracket (Bioland concerns *you*!). But it is with the onset of second-ary education that it will be appropriate, through a fusion of the life sciences and the earth sciences with civic education and the juridical and social sciences, to initiate adolescents to the benefits of a renewal of generations, of a protected human environment, as well as to the demographic requirements of the general progress. One will no longer wait until the last year of high school to comment on Montaigne's essay "Philosophizing is Learning How to Die," or to give as an essay topic the classic "die rather than grow old." Nor the courses in biology to explain that an increase in longevity, as has been demonstrated with mice, is achieved at the expense of the fertility of individuals, so that to delay aging by compensating for hormonal deficiencies results in an increased risk of altering vital functions. A required unit will be designed focusing on the realities of the third age and the disasters of the fourth, with projection of video clips and discussion with the audience. In sum, every resource is to be mobilized so that the ventilation of the existing stock becomes a national cause, as are the battles against cancer and in favor of highway safety. If nothing is to be done within Bioland to inhibit the desires of the transferee, it is altogether appropriate for those desires to have been previously stimulated, educated, and circumscribed by multimedia and interdisciplinary interventions.[*]

If all these conditions are satisfied, our modest proposal, we have no doubt, will be part of the consensus of the circle of Reason.

* * *

Objections have been formulated, more locally, by the ecologists: degradation of the natural

---

[*] This is all the more the case in that in the current state of popular opinion only 76 percent of those older than 65, as opposed to 85 percent on average for the French population, describe themselves as favorable to voluntary death "in the event of a grave and incurable illness accompanied by unbearable suffering."

environment through an accumulation of refuse, assault on the integrity of landscapes by invasive necropolises, non-preservation of traditional sites, soil erosion, risk of epidemics. Ecologists too grow old. And to deplore is not necessarily to argue rationally. And would-be conserver-restorers of the Old World do themselves little credit by insisting doltishly on condemning innovation in the name of the expired reality it supplants. One judges the post-funeral situation using the criteria that predate it. Marble censures the bit, the columbarium (a kind of shantytown for the dead) the computerized necrotheque, the family crypt electronically controlled cremation. All that wailing in the rear-view mirror! Why not rows of tombstones surrounded by cypress trees, with black granite cushions bordered by white tin carnations, and epigraphs engraved in gilt on plates of zinc? Such kitsch is as old as purgatory and the werewolf. One is not far removed from medieval fantasies of decomposing bodies, the insinuating stench of putrefaction, the lugubrious and fetid halo surrounding the grim reaper at the Camposanto. If there is one archaism that will no longer survive in Bioland, as incongruous in its way as emergency medical aid vans and the wailing of ambulance sirens stuck in traffic, it is indeed the costly mess of our urban funerals: the caskets and undertakers, the comings and goings between the funeral home, church, and cemetery (each segment at least an hour long), the laborious lowering of the coffin, with shovels, ropes, and assorted curses, the endless shuffling of feet before, during, and after, and who will travel in the hearse, and who will manage to extricate himself before the end (I'm so sorry, I had a prior engagement), and how is one to get back home afterwards, and where are we going to eat because we're not just going to leave each other like that, are we? We shall leave to the ethnographers of the future the wreaths and chrysanthemums, black ties, obituaries, condolences, inflated costs, widowhood and All Saints Day.... That museum of Arts and Traditions of the Bourgeoisie will soon seem as sinister to us as the posting discovered not too long ago in the hall of the Paris Faculté de Médecine: "Colleague's wife selling complete skeleton."

Yes, Bioland will monitor the follow-up, but in the most rational, systemic, and respectful manner possible. While remaining faithful to its motto: The earth is for the living. And only for them. In administering the non-living, a redistribution of agencies will allow for an optimizing of new compacting procedures.

We have not yet taken full measure of the gain in space, time, and money achieved through the elimination of residues. Once again pride of place should be accorded to the relevant statistics: in 1887, when the Père-Lachaise crematorium was inaugurated, three hundred kilograms of wood were needed to produce, in two hours, 2.7 kilograms of ashes. In 1960, using fuel oil, we were down to one hour and one kilo. In the near future, with lasers, fifteen minutes and 700 grams. The coffin, already replaced by the urn, will tomorrow be supplanted by the package (to be expedited by registered mail or left in a post box) and the day after tomorrow by a sealed plastic bag (for those fetishists reluctant to disperse their ashes on site in a "memory garden." Cost per square meter in our urban centers will no longer allow for either crowding or wastefulness. Thanks to cremation (the choice for 75 percent of all cases), England has already managed to save the equivalent of six hundred soccer fields on its own territory. At present, with container and delivery included, the cost has been calculated at two hundred euros for each effacement-unit. As for the gain in time, it has been observed that since the duration of mourning has traditionally coincided with the time taken for a corpse to decompose, incineration renders it practically pointless.

In addition cremation avoids the fatigue associated with pilgrimages, trips to the grave, and empty periods of "meditation." It comes as no surprise that the most advanced countries are turning increasingly each year to the cremation option: 98.5 percent in Japan, 75.2 percent in Great Britain, around 70 percent in the Scandinavian countries. Bioland should allow Catholic France, with its obsession over investing in stone, to close the gap with its Protestant neighbors. And to definitively convert into private museums and fee-charging parks the antiquated labyrinths of Père-Lachaise and Ménilmontant (which would be the only way to turn a profit on the onerous upkeep, currently assumed by the Division of Parks and Gardens of the City of Paris). In point of fact, the delay will turn out to be beneficial to the extent that Bioland will be able to skip over the residually material and territorial "cremation" stage (with its paper certificate presented to the nearest and dearest, the depositing and transporting of urns) toward a computerized administration of the flow, virtually in real time: labeling and traceability of ashes (for a slight supplementary fee), a data bank consultable with access codes, free information for families so inclined (some will surely remain), and who will be able, for a modest charge, to visualize via screen or CD-ROM memory-images of their dear departed in his or her terminal phase. Beyond such convivial information, biotechnological research allows us to look forward to an optimal use of remains, thereby reconciling the art of arboriculture and life eternal. Following experimental results already achieved at the Royal College of Arts in London, one will be able to select a cell from the mouth of a human subject, extract its DNA, and inject it into the cell of an apple or cherry tree, which upon preservation in solution, will be able to produce, following treatment, a genetically modified transportable seedling. Our British friends have pressed the art of gardening further than us, but acquisition of the patent might inspire the more melancholy among us to plant grandpa (or mom herself) in their garden and watch him (or her) sprout and blossom under one's very window. And perhaps even rediscover at dessert his indefinable aroma by allowing the genetic code of the dearly departed, buried under a slice of apple or a cherry, to melt delectably in one's mouth. Trees would at that point truly have a soul and one would soon encounter a proliferation of ancestral vegetable gardens and orchards in our small farms and—even!—flower pots, sites no longer merely of memory but of genealogical tasting.

The question of determining whether it is appropriate to accord each individual his own personal—and equal—death is, in a democracy, a question for future consideration. If history were not still our code, it would already be *the* question. We do not have a definitive answer—whence our struggle, and the vehemence we feel obliged to bring to the matter. It would be unfortunate if those to whom this report is addressed were to take a theoretical breakthrough for an administrative chore, and what is in fact a prophesy for a profanation. We are seated in the front seat of the vehicle. We are not proposing one more techno-bucolic amusement, a recycling of Empedocles' sandals, or a rear-guard exercise in humanitarianism. Bioland will not take charge of the various laggards of consumer society; it will open up—forgive the grandiloquence—a new chapter in the history of mutants. What must be seen is a fist being raised through the fissure of a very ancient tombstone, which has come close to asphyxiating the species. It is neither for our pleasure (or for theirs) that we will affix a bright red nose to the face of the patriarchs and send clowns in among the incurables (that we all are). Nor because we personally find oak and fir a bit *heavy*, not to say anything of the bronze motorcycle or the gypsum guitar serving as tombstone adornments. Our battle for the freeing up of space, time, and minds must be viewed in the context of the millennial war that we, the living, wage against the dead, and in which, until now, there have been more defeats than victories. "Humanity is composed of more of the dead than the living," said Auguste Comte, the necrophile philosopher little inclined to ecology, who, however mathematically inclined, would never have made it as an accountant. Over two centuries, the society of nations has laid out nine billion corpses along its route. Where are they to be stored? What is to be done with them? At what cost-benefit? Our land is not infinitely extendable. Neither are our memory, archives, libraries, and museums (fortunately all were not writers, sculptors, notaries, or painters). Are we not saturated with pyramids, mausolea, catacombs, cenotaphs, necropolises, stela, cemeteries, tombstones, recumbent statues, and calvaries? Do we want to turn the planet into a mole-hill? A Pompeii without end? For every new ossuary will we need a polder?

The moss-covered slab that prevents us from breathing and impedes our march forward toward the light comes in three different thicknesses: the elderly, books, and the dead. Those complicitous anachronisms form the conservation society which we will never overcome if we fail to attack on all three fronts. We cannot fight separately against the tyranny of the dead and that of books. We will not stop the invasion of our airports, shopping centers, and electoral lists by advanced age without reducing the space accorded to corpses in our Europolises, bookstores in our population centers, and stories in our lives. There is something of the ghoul in the page-swallower and of the novel-reader in the stroller through cemeteries. Interment, reading, and wistfulness have a common interest. This is something the Americans have understood; according to a number of studies, they bury and read less and less. Between 1982 and 2002, the number of readers has declined in the United States by 10 percent. One American out of two no longer reads books. And half the rest read only digests. The New World is leading the Old in the right direction, but it would be presumptuous to assume that the battle has been won. There are still fossils around who insist on teaching the children of Europe Latin and Greek. As well as future embalmees who demand from Brussels translations from English to Dutch, Italian, or French.

In brief, we are dealing with nothing less than forging a civilization in which laying to final rest, conversing willingly with the old, and reading

War and Peace in its entirety will be antiquarian amusements. Better still: in which death itself will be a thing of the past. If that is not an innovation, one is hard put to see what is.

No doubt, one does not start from zero. For years now, our cities have been casting their refuse *extra-muros*, under highway connectors. Our cellars are full. One has to go to Palermo to find mummies perched on balconies, decked in ribbons. Malodorous or not, of flesh or paper, bodies all the more physical for the stench of their decay can now be made virtual. Their upkeep is costly and they travel rather poorly. Once computerized, books, like incinerated corpses, wander and are dispersed more effectively. In the wind, by sea or in pixels. How are we to sell off three-dimensional bodies, no longer fit for exhibition, production, or pleasure? Who can no longer be perched on a bike, in a stadium, on a stage or a bed, who can't dance, undress themselves, sing, pedal, grab a microphone, score a point, or win a race? By helping them take leave on tip-toe. "Everything is to disappear." And let us not regret the time when a son, friend, or sister themselves undertook, with hesitant gestures, to awkwardly prepare the corpse. Our morticians do better. We should rejoice in the fact that the "death mask," in wax or plaster, has become incongruous, and the "death bed photo," that paper mold, prohibited. Our ancestors went through their death throes rather grandiosely. We shall take leave discreetly. The obscure tomes of yesteryear have less and less to say to the young; and our dearest deceased leave us like "books one no longer opens." We no longer have much to say to each other, for lack of a common language. Absence has lost its resonance. One no longer finds epitaphs on recent tombstones, and the "in memory of," which only recently replaced the more confident *requiescat in pace*, is disappearing in turn. Useless. Like the simple past tense and the imperfect subjunctive in the newspapers. Here lies no one. Resting nowhere. What we need is action. A democracy owes it to itself to live day by day. Only the future can make humans equal, peaceful, and convivial. Once their past remains stuck to their skin, they will rip each other apart. It is our moral responsibility to prevent resurgences and wipe the slate clean of all residues of prehistory, so that man himself may become a perpetual springtime, with neither winter nor autumn.

We are already working free of the old world by stifling the voice of the doddering individual dormant within us. He is a shadow in the brilliant sunlight, which blurs the message and does damage to authentic life: continuous news, advertising, opinion polls, cars, penalty shots, and portable phones. The grinches who denounce the much mentioned "symptoms of dehumanization" fail to see that a pioneer mode of humanity is emerging beneath our eyes, in which the mumblers, blushers, and perplexed will no longer have any place. We must love it because nothing will stop it. For *it* is stronger. As a precaution, certain words should be avoided from the outset, such as fragility, melancholy, secret, grace, ugliness, mourning, embarrassment, kindness, poetry, chagrin, mystery, slowness, nostalgia, silence. They feel old. Henceforth every individual should train, and without delay, to go directly to what counts: what use is it? What is it worth? How big an audience? And: How long does it last?

It will be appreciated that our proposal can move things forward. The fact that it is in advance of its time will not prevent enlightened sectors of public opinion from latching on to it, indeed from enriching it with a thousand useful suggestions.

* * *

In conclusion, allow me, *Monsieur le chef de service*, and even if immodesty is not customary in administrative spheres, to indulge in one final indication of a personal nature. The author of this report is sixty-three years old. He has taken his retirement and taken leave of all his official functions, which, moreover, were modest. Neither a member of an Academy, nor a decorated official, nor particularly wealthy, he has already received whatever inheritance was his, and learned how to distinguish between silver-plate and silver. In this regard (and in several others), he enjoys all the conditions required for being among the very first to benefit from the hygienic amenities of Bioland, which will be inscribed on his agenda, to be sure, before his seventieth birthday. Aware that the upcoming generations are in greater need of witnesses than of speeches, and of men of action than of authors, he has not relinquished the hope of taking part, when the time comes, in its implementation, and of spreading its blessings, with his own example, among his invalid brothers.